NOGGLE STONES BOOK 1 1/2: BUGBEAR'S TRAVELS

by
Wil Radcliffe

Artwork
By
Ernie Colón

Noggle Stones Book 1 1/2: Bugbear's Travels

by Wil Radcliffe

Copyright Ernest William Radcliffe 2013

Published by R Corners Publishing

ISBN: 0615894909

R Corners Publishing
Coldwater, MI
USA

www.nogglestones.com

For Mom & Dad.

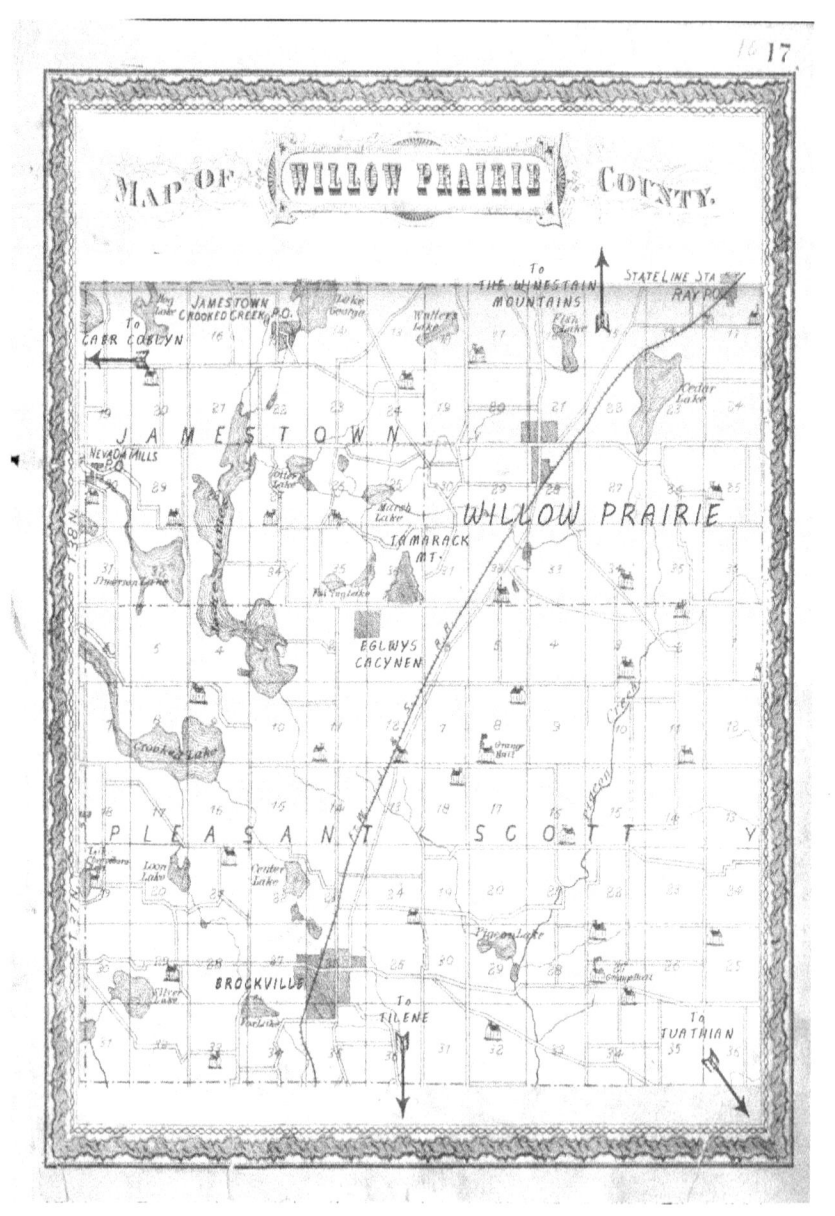

MAP OF WILLOW PRAIRIE COUNTY.

Table of Contents

Bugbear's Journal

Day of the Dim Possum, Year of the Dappled Beetle,
Age of the Unstrung Harp
September 18, 1899 - by human reckoning

It has been but one week since I left Willow Prairie. I have yet to uncover any evidence of this subtler power mentioned by Cron. While I suppose it is rather early in my investigations, and therefore not entirely unexpected that I should find myself confronted with false leads, red herrings, and empty answers, I nonetheless struggle to keep my brain from overheating in agitation. Fortunately, I was able to rescue several books from Willow Prairie's library. Chief among them is a history of the Nagonene. It is with this tome that I have been soothing my impatient mind, caressing its nervous nooks and crannies with all manner of intriguing facts and hidden histories.

One discovery I have made is that while the markings on the bow Riley found are indeed Nagonene, more accurately they are from a division of the Nagonene military caste known as the Migatwik. The Migatwik were a particularly fearsome regiment, reportedly Reginald's most elite and trusted warriors. But Reginald did not gain their allegiance easily.

Legend has it they tasked him with seven deadly quests, each involving the recovery of a certain rare item or ingredient. Reginald faced and conquered each quest, returning with the required prizes. It was with these rare items of ghost wood, onager pelt, wourmboggle venom, jotun boar bristle, banshee whisper, ogre moss, and tylluan feather, that the Nagonene constructed their legendary bows. It is said these weapons are eternal and unbreakable, meaning the one Riley carries could well be a relic from the age of Whittlegrip and Reginald.

It is worth noting that despite Reginald's acceptance of contemporary steel arms and armor, the Nagonene and Migatwik were steadfast and consistent in their use of more natural weapons such as flint-tipped arrows and tomahawks. Indeed, it is this very fact which made them so deadly. While armored knights would cause quite a ruckus during a sneak attack, the Migatwik could stalk in unheard and unseen... like ghosts. The chronicles say the fearful reputation of the Migatwik was so potent that if certain Coranieid generals heard even the faintest rumor of Reginald's approach, rather than face the nightmare of a Migatwik assault they would abandon the battlefield before a single arrow was shot.

If only these brave warriors were here now. Reginald's heir could use their peerless prowess in the coming battles. And yet, I am reminded that even as Reginald founded Willow Prairie, the Nagonene and Migatwik were with him. Perhaps that fierce warrior blood has been diluted some by time and complacency... but the spark may yet be there... may yet be ignited. After all, the men and women of Willow Prairie fought valiantly against the Shadow Smith and his hordes. I suspect their Nagonene ancestors would be proud. Prouder still of what they yet might accomplish under Manchester's guidance.

SHADOW PLAYS

The goblin's hands moved in graceful arcs and turns that belied his stubby fingers. The shadows danced upon the wall, following his movements and playing their parts in his gentle production.

The small crowd watched with amazement as the goblin's tale came to life before their eyes. Monsters attacked peasants. Sorcerers conjured spirits. Heroes overthrew despots. So many images moving in dark silhouettes... so real and yet wrought by only moonlight and a strange little man's dexterous hands.

The goblin finished and bowed deeply. "And that, my dear friends, is the tale of how I defeated the dreaded Shadow Smith whilst reuniting the worlds of fey and humankind. And now to show your appreciation you may place your coins in the cup of Bugbear, the greatest goblin scholar and minstrel in the Scatter Lands."

Some of the villagers meandered on, having enjoyed the tale but not the request. Others stayed at the street corner, tossing their coins and trinkets eagerly into Bugbear's dented tin cup. They laughed and smiled. Although they did not seem used to Bugbear's strange race, they found him at the least quaint and at the most delightful.

"You are most kind," Bugbear said. " The next performance shall commence shortly."

Suddenly a young man and woman burst through the crowd. Their eyes bulged wide and wild as their gangly, rag-clad bodies pushed, pried, and plowed a path through the bewildered and outraged townsfolk.

Several armed guards, layered head to toe in pale green armor, rampaged after the refugees. Upon their chests were cryptic runes, and one of them carried a banner with a black raven crest.

"The Coranieid?" Bugbear said as he dodged the rampage. "But they're extinct!"

The humans themselves seemed less inclined towards disbelief and more aligned with terror. "Dis Pater's men!" one exclaimed with panic.

The villagers scattered like chickens fleeing the butcher's blade. Doors slammed. Shutters closed. Locks bolted. Soon Bugbear stood alone before his performance wall, the fading sounds of armored footfalls his only company.

"Dis Pater?" Bugbear said to himself. "There's a familiar name." He lay a finger upon his chin. "Dis Pater, Dis Pater, Dis Pater." He mulled over the name a few more moments in his mind before shrugging and taking up his cup of offerings. "Bah!" he scoffed as he found an odd looking stone with a leather strap in his coffers. "I'd rather they give me nothing at all than worthless trinkets like this." With a casual sigh Bugbear placed the oddity in his vest pocket and gathered up the small satchel which held his belongings. Then with a skip and a jump he made out for the local tavern.

The streets of the quaint village vibrated with dying echoes. A pale cloud drifted over the moon, spraying the air with gray flecks of shadow. Bugbear suppressed a growing sense of dread, a peculiar feeling that unpleasant things awaited. He doubled his pace and steadied his breath, for even a goblin had cause to fear when the Coranieid were about.

The Coranieid... their name was as ancient as terror itself. Some called them "the poisoners". Others claimed they were the devil's own. But whatever their origins, whatever their goals, the Coranieid had haunted the dreams and realities of every race since the dawn of time. That was until the humans rose up all those centuries ago, before the Great Sundering of the world, and after the reign of the Dragon-Kings. It was said that the Mumblers of Antioch, those mysterious and wise human mages, placed a curse upon the Coranieid making them allergic to all reality. The Mumblers used the true names of all things in their spell... except for a mysterious relic from ages gone by for which there was no true name; and the Dragons, who had long since evolved into pure spirit, leaving only their empty shells behind. The curse proved devastating. Soon the Coranieid faded from existence until it seemed there was naught left of them but shadows and whispered nightmare tales.

But now they had returned. For Bugbear had recognized their banners and crests from ancient tomes he had perused in the Library of Antioch itself. But how had this dead race risen? And why? Perhaps Bugbear's own actions of two years past (that spectacular adventure in which he and his companions destroyed the tyrannical Shadow Smith and reunited the worlds of human and fey) rebirthed the foul Coranieid. And perhaps now they sought to destroy all which could destroy them... including Bugbear himself!

Suddenly Bugbear's goose-pimpling fears were realized. A hand grabbed him tightly about the arm, pulling him down into a filth filled ditch. "You must stop him."

Bugbear whirled about, his pug face contorted into a mask of fright. "Away from me, unclean wretch!" he blurted.

"Listen to me," the battered warrior pleaded as he took Bugbear by the shoulders. "I am dying. The others attacked me when I questioned the Dis Pater." He pointed to a small hole in his battered, soiled armor. "My Dragon-skin armor is no longer whole. I have been contaminated... the Curse of the Mumblers takes me."

Bugbear slid from the creature's grasp. "What do you want me to do then, Coranieid scum? Make your funeral arrangements?"

"Silence your mocking tongue, goblin!" the warrior hissed. "You must stop the Dis Pater! With their armor the others are too strong for the humans. But you are a goblin. You can move in places they cannot. You can think around reality and find hidden truths. Even we Coranieid, as much as we hate your kind, respect your talents for sabotage. That has been foremost in my mind since I first saw you come into town. You're the only hope."

"And why should I stop this Dis Pater?" Bugbear asked.

"Who is he that he poses such a threat?"

"He seeks ultimate power," the armored figure whispered. "At first it was a quest to cure of us the Mumbler's Curse... a pursuit of noble intent. But now it has corrupted into a lust for domination." The Coranieid warrior's voice began to fade. "You must keep him from finding...." Then with a dull clatter the armor caved in on dead space.

Cautiously Bugbear poked at the debris with a stick taken from nearby. Lifeless ashes stirred beneath the green armor, but nothing more was seen. "Curious," Bugbear muttered. "The Coranieid must have fashioned this armor to protect them from the curse. Being of Dragon flesh, it would keep them safe. Perhaps a small group of them has been in hiding all these centuries. But why emerge now? What is it that this Dis Pater seeks?" The goblin scholar's head puttered from side to side, like a tea pot coming to a boil. His mind struggled through the thick bog of mystery. But then everything cleared with one sudden, bright, white realization. "Oh well! None of my concern! Off to the tavern now!" With that, Bugbear clambered out of the ditch and waddled down the street, an off-key tune trailing from his whistling lips.

The tavern choked and sputtered with distasteful life. Ruffians, derelicts, and blackguards sat about in staggered clumps, their eyes dull and blank from excessive sin. Sober they might have found the little goblin that waddled into their lives alarming, but drunk as they were, Bugbear provided only a momentary excuse to grunt before slipping back into delirium.

"A cup of hot water, my good man!" Bugbear piped to the barkeep as he climbed upon a stool.

"You that little shadow making beastie I heard about?" the grizzled man replied.

"Indeed," Bugbear beamed. "Now, a cup of hot water, please."

"What you want that for?"

"Why, to brew my tea, of course."

"We got tea aplenty," the barkeep glowered. "You can have some of ours."

"I'm sorry," Bugbear said. "I carry my own special brand. Yours, no doubt, would upset my delicate constitution."

The barkeep then grumbled a few inaudible curses and thundered through the swinging doors, back into the kitchen area.

"Disagreeable creature," Bugbear muttered. Then with a sigh he reached into his vest pocket for his tin of precious tea. "Hello, what's this?" Instead his awkward fingers fumbled upon the odd trinket someone had thrown into his beggar's cup. He removed the object and studied it in the tavern's dim light. Milk white and shaped like a stretched out egg... that was how he saw it. At the small end a leather strap had been attached, perhaps to turn it into a necklace or even a headband. Indeed the trinket was odd.

"Your cup of water," the barkeep said as he slid a mug before Bugbear.

"Ah!" Bugbear said. "Very good! Thank you, my good man!" The goblin quickly shoved the trinket back into his vest pocket and removed his tin of tea. Gingerly he sprinkled the tea leaves into the steaming mug, stirring them gently with his pinky before licking said digit with a satisfied lip-smack. "Ah! Perfect! Perfect! Now, would you happen to have any pasty cakes? Tea simply is not the same without pasty cakes."

"Just finish your tea and get out," he replied. "You be upsetting my regulars."

Bugbear turned about and scanned the room of ruffians. Half of them had drunk themselves into unconsciousness, and the other half looked like they were envying the first half. "Yes, I can see how they might find my sobriety upsetting. Very well, barkeep. I shall hastily drink my tea and risk hiccups. However, I require lodgings for the night. Do you offer rooms for rent?"

"I got rooms. You got money?"

"Money?" Bugbear blurted. "Blather and bother! I have no need for money! I am a minstrel and performer! It is tradition for persons of my standing to be offered free lodgings!"

"I'll have none of that, little man!" the barkeep spat. "I hear you been making quite a bit of money with your shadows! You can afford to pay for a room!"

"And you could afford to learn some manners, you babbling brute!" Bugbear blurted. "Have you no respect for tradition?"

"Yes. I have a great deal of respect for such traditions as, oh, let's say, paying for lodgings."

The goblin sputtered and fumed as he reached into his many pockets rummaging about for coinage. After some fussing and fumbling Bugbear finally withdrew three gold coins. "I trust this shall suffice?"

"It'll do," the barkeep said as he scooped the coins into his greasy, sausage-link hands. "There's a room at the top of the stairs, third door on the left. If you want a bath it's two gold extra."

"Goblin's don't bathe. We're too clever to get dirty. Thank you very much." And with a scowl, scoot, and scamper, Bugbear was up the stairs.

Sleep was dreadful and plodding for Bugbear that night. True, the feather bed was comfortable enough, but the warnings of the dying Coranieid kept flitting through his head. And the strange young people who broke up his shadow play... they ran in and out of his thoughts as well. He tossed about in his bed like a fitful dog swimming in a sea of fleas.

"They say the best cure for insomnia is a clean conscience," a voice whispered from across the room.

"Who?" Bugbear exclaimed bolting upright.

"'Tis an admirer of the great Bugbear," the voice continued.

"Show yourself, taunter!" Bugbear shouted to the vague shadows and hissing darkness. He reached over and with thick, fumbling fingers lit the lamp on his night stand.

An eerie, gray-tinted, lifeless luminance filled the room. And the Coranieid stood revealed, several of them standing tall and broad shouldered in their dragon-skin armor. They held captive the two youngsters who had been so prominent in Bugbear's concerns. But most noticeable was the bold creature who stood in their midst like an oak in a forest of saplings. As did the Coranieid he wore the dragon-skin armor, yet his sprouted spikes and thorns and spires and horns. He seemed some primordial god... some ancient force of nature.

"The Dis Pater, I presume," Bugbear said, trying to hide his fears.

"Indeed," the being replied. "It is a genuine pleasure to meet you, Bugbear. I had heard of your spectacular shadow plays even before you set foot in this humble village."

Bugbear could feel cold, steel eyes boring into his soul. He pulled the covers up to his chin, peering at the Dis Pater with eyes narrowed by suspicion. "You did not come here to discuss shadow plays, of that I've no doubt. What do you want?"

"Of course," the Dis Pater said with an apologetic bow. "I have forgotten how impatient and curious goblins can be. These children have taken something from me. I had hired them, you see, to pilfer a small item for me from a merchant here in the village. They did so, but, as is often the case with humans, they let greed get in the way of good sense. They actually thought to hold the object for ransom... to badger me into paying them more. Very unethical, I thought. But then they are thieves after all."

"It seems you have captured them," Bugbear observed. "So

I fail to see how this affects me."

"Well, the boy here... Darius, I believe is his name... he claims to have tossed the trinket into your cup while being pursued by my men. It was not difficult to trace your steps, as you are the only goblin in these parts and your comings and goings attract a considerable amount of attention... as well as animosity. In fact, the owner of this establishment was only too happy to allow us entry to your room."

Bugbear swallowed hard as he remembered the dying Coranieid's warnings and childhood stories of Coranieidian cruelty "What exactly did this 'trinket' look like?"

"It was a milk white stone, very smooth and unblemished," the Dis Pater said.

"I... I have seen no such stones," Bugbear lied.

"So it seems these children are liars as well as thieves." Slowly the Dis Pater slid his sword from its sheath. "The girl's name is Gwenhwyvar. I believe it is Welsh for 'white spirit'. Indeed her skin is quite fair, is it not? A lovely girl. Almost Coranieid-like in beauty." He placed the sword gently against the girl's cheek. "Perhaps if I threaten violence against Gwenhwyvar, her suitor will tell me the truth."

"But I did tell you the truth!" Darius exclaimed. "The little man has the stone!"

"Well, liars or not, you have to admire their persistence," the Dis Pater chuckled. "A shame to waste such beauty at the edge of a sword."

Gwenhwyvar looked to Bugbear with pleading eyes. Her

soft, young body quivered with terror. Her throat quaked with barely audible sobs. Her brow dripped with perspiration.

"By the hoary beard of Oberon!" Bugbear suddenly exclaimed. "A wourmboggle slithers from behind you!"

The Coranieid turned about with alarm to see a serpentine shape slinking across the wall. Black as ink the form seemed to reach at them with waving tentacles and twisting arms. The Coranieid drew their blades and advanced on the oddity, leaving the youths poorly guarded. Even the Dis Pater took his sword from Gwenhwyvar's cheek and directed it toward the loathsome shadow.

Bugbear pulled his secretive hands from in front of the lamp and leapt from his bed. He snatched up his coat of many pockets, ran to the prisoners, and tore them from the warriors' loosened grips. Then all three disappeared out the door and down the hall.

"He has tricked us with his bothersome shadows!" the Dis Pater raged. "After them!"

Bugbear led the humans down a set of back steps and into an alley. "Follow me, you floundering fools!" he ordered as he set out through the maze of streets. They scurried over decaying bridges and loose cobble paths, zigzagging around high spired churches and straw thatched cottages, careening through brown puddles of water and neatly trimmed hedges. Finally, in the secretive fashion of fugitives, they entered a windmill on the outskirts of the village.

"Bar the door," Bugbear said as he sat upon the floor. He

rummaged through his over-sized coat pockets and removed a large, yellowed tome. "The Gray Book of Antioch," Bugbear hissed with delight. "I have some reading to do."

"Reading?" the boy scoffed. "Those Coranieid could burst through that door any minute. We should be planning a defense, not reading!"

"Reading brings knowledge," Bugbear explained softly. "Knowledge is the greatest defense of all." And with a relishing smile he began to flit through his precious volume of lore. Quickly he rifled through the dried parchment pages, skimming along the wise wordings of wizards past, glancing through the pretentious ponderings of long dead philosophers, until finally settling on a particularly relevant page.

"Of all the beggar's cups in the city, you had to toss the stone into a goblin's," Gwenhwyvar sighed.

"I've had enough out of you, Gwenhwyvar!" Darius countered. "At least I wasn't the one who waved the stone under the Dis Pater's nose thinking to lure him out and barter with him."

"You're the one who got us mixed up with the heartless fiend in the first place!" she yelled. "My mother was right about you all along! You're nothing but trouble!"

"Well, at least my brand of trouble has kept food in your belly and clothes on your back!"

"What good is food and clothing when your head's on an Coranieidian pike?"

"Aha!" Bugbear erupted with fact finding pleasure. He

held up the book he had been studying. "This is the history of the fall of the Coranieid. It tells of how the great Coranieidian king Eluned used the power of a forgotten relic centuries ago to fight off human hordes threatening his kingdom. There's even an elaborate woodcut here depicting the event." His stubby goblin finger pointed out the intricate picture. "Anyhow, it goes on to tell how during the final battle, the wise Mumblers of Antioch used their arcane powers to curse the Coranieidian empire. As the Coranieid faltered under the oppression of the curse, the human armies stormed the capital city and took possession of the stone. Apparently Eluned had feared using the stone's power to its fullest."

"I bet you the Dis Pater won't be so shy," Gwenhwyvar muttered.

"Since that time the stone has passed down through human hands from generation to generation, from one conqueror's treasuries to another's," Bugbear continued. "Obviously human's lack the discipline to use its powers... and even in the Coranieidian population I imagine only royalty can utilize the stone effectively." Bugbear suddenly cocked his head with interest and looked deeply at the picture. "Curious," he whispered.

Pounding and Coranieidian curses met at the door.

"They've found us!" Darius panicked.

"Hold them off," Bugbear ordered as he pulled a magnifying glass from his coat. "I've found something quite interesting and potentially vital." His wide saucer eye studied the woodcut intently.

"Would you stop reading that ratty old book!" Gwenhwyvar yelled as she pressed against the door.

"What more is there to learn?" Darius asked as he began bracing boards and beams between the floor and door.

Bugbear ignored them. His eyes skimmed over the rampaging barbarians, ran along the noble Coranieidian ranks, and studied the defiant figure of King Eluned. The Coranieidian leader's arm stretched out over the humans, beams of terrific energy lancing out from the pure, smooth, unblemished stone. Bugbear knew from previous study that the Mumbler scholars and artists who scribed the Gray Book of Antioch never embellished. Their woodcuts were meticulous in detail and fact. Therefore when he noted the simple, unadorned stone depicted in Eluned's naked hand, and then compared it to the simple stone that dangled from his own hand by its leather strap, he became aware of a most ironic situation.

"Stand aside," Bugbear said as he pushed his way to the door, strewing the boards and beams away and undoing the latch.

The door flew open, revealing a hissing cadre of heavily armored Coranieid.

"We surrender," Bugbear said with an agreeable nod.

The Dis Pater pushed his way to the front of the Coranieid. "The stone, if you please."

"Of course," Bugbear said as he pulled the object from his vest pocket. He placed it in the Dis Pater's dragon-gloved hand.

The Coranieidian guards filed in and recaptured their prisoners.

"I am disappointed in you, Bugbear," the Dis Pater said as he admired the long sought relic. "Usually goblins provide more sport before yielding their treasures." The Dis Pater removed his gauntlet and pressed the stone into his naked palm. "And now you and the children shall be the first to fall before the might of the new Coranieidian empire! For the first time in 5000 years a Coranieid of the royal house wields the great stone of power!" He held the stone aloft as brilliant rays of energy spread out. He removed his great war helmet and shook out his long mane of silver hair. Gray eyes smiled with insanity and a perfect mouth opened to let out a soulless laugh.

The other Coranieid released the captives and knelt down before their glorified lord.

Darius and Gwenhwyvar rushed to Bugbear's side, finding him the only source of comfort in an increasingly uncomfortable situation.

Bugbear watched on, his eyes wide and eagle like. He felt the pinpricks of anticipation along his spine.

And then, like indiscriminate bolts of lightning, the energy began striking down the Coranieid. Slicing out angrily, spitting bitter rays, flinging tongues of fire, the stone turned and twisted in the Dis Pater's hand. Soon all his followers lay decimated, piles of lifeless ash.

"What is this?" he gasped. His glorious hair fell out in

clumps. His clean, bronze skin began to wrinkle and fall away in pale chunks. He slumped to the ground, burdened by the weight of decay. "What have you done?" he hissed to Bugbear.

"I have given you the nameless relic," Bugbear replied. He snatched the smoldering object from the Dis Pater's weak grasp. "It is the exact same stone your ancestor used to fight off the human hordes all those centuries ago." Bugbear dangled the stone before his enemy's fading eyes. "Except that when the stone fell into human hands something was added. A handy little leather strap. Humans are always loosing things, you know. I think the strap was a very worthwhile adornment. Don't you?"

"I have been contaminated!" the Dis Pater screeched. "The strap was human made!" And with one final, raging moan the Dis Pater faded into oblivion.

Bugbear plopped the handy trinket back into his pocket. He looked over to Gwenhwyvar and Darius, his mouth split into a demented grin. "You know, I believe that there is something to be gained from this little adventure."

Epilogue

The small crowd watched with amazement as the goblin's tale came to life before their eyes. Coranieid warriors stormed the streets. Human thieves prowled the alleys. And goblin scholars buried ancient nightmares. So many images moving in dark silhouettes... so real and yet wrought by only moonlight and a strange little man's dexterous hands.

The goblin finished and bowed deeply. "And that, my dear friends, is the tale of how I defeated the nightmarish Coranieid whilst saving two hapless human thieves from their own foolish ambitions. And now to show your appreciation you may place your coins in the cup of Bugbear, the greatest goblin scholar and minstrel in the Scatter Lands."

"Well, this is just fabulous," Darius said with a sarcastic drawl as he and Gwenhwyvar nudged through the crowd of coin-tossing spectators. "After all the trouble we went through, you're the one who makes money from it!"

"Now, now, my boy," Bugbear said. "No need to be jealous of my genius! I'm willing to share a few of my earnings with you and your charming companion. However, the stone shall have to remain in my possession. It's too dangerous to be floating about."

"We'll take what we can get," Gwenhwyvar said as she began rummaging through Bugbear's cup full of coins.

"Here now!" Bugbear blurted. "I said take some, not the entire collection!"

"What's this?" Darius said as he plucked up an odd looking bauble.

Bugbear snapped to alertness as he snatched the item from the startled boy. "Oh my! Oh mercy! Oh my mercy!" Bugbear studied the object with a magnifying glass, his expression growing ever more frantic as he gazed upon each facet. "Do you realize what this is? 'Tis the Broach of Lleu Llaw Gyffes! A most ancient relic, sought by power-mad despots throughout the centuries! Legend has it that...."

Before the goblin could complete his sentence, Darius and Gwenhwyvar spun about and tore through the crowd, screeches of terror trailing from their lips.

Bugbear watched the youths scatter, shrugged, and went back to his examination of the relic. "Oh, gracious me! This isn't the Broach of Lleu Llaw Gyffes! 'Tis a button come loose from my coat! Blather and bother! And me without a sewing kit!"

And with a mad titter, the goblin commenced counting his cup full of coins.

The End

Neither Here's Nor There's

Dead silence. That is the best way to describe it. No. Stone dead silence. That is more accurate. For the entire assemblage was still, from the front row dignitaries of the grand outdoor amphitheater, to the far off spectators on the hillside picnic blankets. All eyes were fixed upon two figures... one - Professor De Sarno - standing defiantly at the podium, the other - Bugbear the goblin - poised menacingly at the foot of the stage. Each glared at the other with a hatred reserved only for the most despised of enemies. Each breathed with the deep, labored gasps of impassioned warriors ready to rip, rend, and ruin for their beloved causes. Each was a scholar defending his theories... and a deadlier menace can seldom be found!

"Get off of that stage," Bugbear hissed. "One of your limited intellect does not deserve the honor of addressing such a noble gathering."

"I told you before, you bothersome beggar," De Sarno said with a steady, determined tone, "it is a colloquialism."

"It is intolerable!" the goblin shouted. "Scholars do not rely upon common expressions! Ours is the language of Kings!"

"You tell that nadredd!" an old woman cackled from the gallery, the only observer bold enough to comment on the proceedings... much to the discomfort of those around her.

"All I said was 'There's many reasons why we should look to our own minds for answers to the questions around us,'" De Sarno said.

"'There's' is a contraction of 'there' and 'is'!" Bugbear screeched. "So in essence you said 'There is many reasons...!' Where as a proper gentleman would have said 'There are many reasons!'"

"But you miss the point of my thesis on the nature of perception and reality if..."

"I miss nothing, 'Professor' De Sarno!" the goblin interrupted. "Regardless of your so-called revolutionary theories - which sound for all the world like a shallow plagiarism of my own research into Non-Logical Thought - you cannot be allowed to deliver them in such an undisciplined manner. Reality and perception? Bah! Don't you realize that if reality is based upon perception, then perception is based upon information, and information is based upon language! Therefore, if one's language is flawed, then so is one's information, which in turn affects perception, which then destroys reality!"

"He's right!" the old woman interrupted again. "Let's flog the cretin!"

Another taller, younger woman in a hooded cloak stood up from her seat near the stage. Actually, she seemed something more than a woman. Her features were flawless. Her stance was dynamic. Her manner was haughty. And her voice... her voice was like a thousand tranquil rivers of honey. "With all due respect to Masters Bugbear and De Sarno, this debate resolves nothing. I suggest we adjourn the seminar for a two hour recess to allow tempers to cool. Agreed?"

The tall woman looked to Bugbear and De Sarno. Each pulled his gaze from the other long enough to nod in agreement.

"As you are a Royal Arbitrator, I shall agree," De Sarno said.

"As shall I," Bugbear said. "However, I expect an official petition to be circulated amongst the council members calling for censure against Professor De Sarno."

"Preposterous!" De Sarno erupted. "Where do you get off making such demands?"

"You seem to have respect for one of the King's Arbitrators," Bugbear said, motioning to the tall woman. "Should you not have the same respect for the King's Advisor… who also happens to be me? And is this scholarly convention not sponsored by the King? And does that not make me the King's official representative at this convention?"

De Sarno shook, veins bulging upon his bald scalp, and flesh flushing fuchsia. "And so you shall silence my groundbreaking theories on the nature of reality and perception merely due to a slip of the tongue?"

"Indeed," Bugbear said. "That is my intent."

"Infernal goblin troublemaker!"

"Hmmmmm," Bugbear said with an arched brow and thoughtful stroke of his mutton chops. "Perhaps I should add 'racism' to the good Professor's list of offenses?" Then with a smug smirk, sarcastic salute, and unsavory snort Bugbear waddled from the outdoor amphitheater and onto the streets of Tiline.

The council of scholars muttered amongst themselves. The most brilliant minds of seven races, the keenest intellects of thirty city-states, the greatest philosophers of all the Scatter Lands, and not a one of them fully understood what had just occurred. After all, most had simply come to the convention for the free truffles and tea.

"I bet you two hundred coppers that the little one ends up biting the big one on the ankle before this is all over," the old woman said to a group of the uneasy truffle-eaters and tea-swillers.

De Sarno trembled and tottered as he watched his hated rival leave. He twisted a ring on his pinkie, and as he toyed with the bauble, his mood seemed to lighten... as though some glowing ember of inspiration ignited his brain.

The streets bubbled, thrummed, hummed, and vibrated with excitement. The marketplace of Tiline enjoyed a particular fame throughout the Scatter Lands. After the Great Reunification of the Human and Fey Worlds some five years ago, Tiline became second only to the Kingdom of Willow Prairie as the most integrated and prominent center of commerce in the realm. Their marketplace boasted the boldest dwarven metalcrafts, the most advanced human inventions, the finest aes dana silks, and the rarest goblin writings. During a casual walk through the marketplace of Tiline, one could see everything from buffalo rifles and two-handed swords to sorcerer's wands and wizards' staves, and from buttered muffins and silver teapots to live rats and better mousetraps. Some called it one of the Fourteen Wonders of the Scatter Lands. Others called it a waste of good real estate.

"Of course I am right," Bugbear whispered to himself as he browsed through the wares of a parchment vender. "Those fools on the council should be kissing my feet and proclaiming my sainthood for stopping De Sarno from grammatically butchering all of existence!"

"Why are you talking to yourself?" the fat parchment merchant asked the goblin.

"Because I'd like an intelligent conversation for a change!" Bugbear exploded with flailing arms.

"You shouldn't ought to have yelled at me like that," the merchant said as he glared down at him.

"None of that concerns you!" Bugbear said. "Step lively, my good man! I require service! Sterling service! Fetch me your finest parchment! Your finest, I say!"

The fat merchant stared dumbly at the irate goblin. Then slowly he removed a bundle of crisp parchments from behind the stand. "Here's my best parchments. They're imported from..."

"'Here's'?" Bugbear exploded as he swatted the papers

from the startled merchant's hand. "'Here's'? Why you festering pustule of ignorance! It's neither here's nor there's! Neither here's nor there's! Do you understand me? Do you?"

"No," the merchant said with a dumb, blank stare. "Not really."

"Bah!" The goblin stormed away, ranting and chanting to any who would hear, "Neither here's nor there's! Neither here's nor there's!"

In his haste and rage he spilled into a particular man and soon became entangled with him in a series of elegant rugs hung upon poles and wires.

"Bothersome booger!" the man yelled, his words slurred by alcohol. "I've been saving for five months to buy this rug! If you've damaged it...."

"Bah!" Bugbear scoffed. "Rugs and people... always under foot!" The goblin extracted himself from the tangle, gave the man a sharp glare, and once again set upon his way.

As can be imagined, Bugbear did not care much for the city. Even small towns such as Tiline made him feel dirty and harried. And so days ago when he was on his way to the convention and he found a quaint stream just outside of town, he made a small camp there rather than rely upon the inefficiencies and hazards of a room at an inn.

And that is where he was now, lying upon that grassy bank, letting the sounds of the gentle, trickling waters ease him into a thought-empty slumber. He let the tensions, rages, and frustrations of earlier fall away like a dead husk... leaving only peace, contentment, and...

"Murderous scumbag!"

Bugbear's eyes fluttered open just in time to shut as a rifle butt slammed into his pug face.

In that sanity-snapping moment the thought-empty slumber was gone, replaced with a vile, violent unconsciousness pulsating with worrisome rot, bewildering buzzing, and miserable madness.

"I never imagined you would take it this far," came a familiar, stern, yet melodic voice.

Bugbear forced his eyes open. The dull pain throbbed through his head as he rose from a small cot in a small jail cell. Outside the bars he saw the Royal Arbitrator. "What are you yammering about?" the goblin asked.

"De Sarno," she said. "They found him dead... poisoned. The coroner says it was underdark root, a rare herb found only in Roundabout Wood... which is where you hail from."

"This is utter nonsense!" Bugbear protested. "You just ended your sentence with a preposition!"

"I would be less concerned with grammar and more concerned with your defense."

"And why is it you are here?" Bugbear said as he glared at the woman, waddling from his cot to a small wash basin. "Are you to lead me to the gallows for this crime I did not commit?"

"No," the woman said. "I have made arrangements for

your release."

"Ah! Excellent! Excellent! You have convinced the constable that I am innocent!"

"No," the woman said. "I have used my influence as Royal Arbitrator to declare 'Iawn Rhydd Cwestiwn' on your behalf."

"Right of Free Question," Bugbear said. "Very good. That means I shall be free to assemble my own defense against these slanderous charges."

"Yes. But I shall be your guardian in that time. Any attempts to escape and I shall be forced to kill you."

"One bad death deserves another, eh?" Bugbear said with a sarcastic smirk as he finished toweling off his face. "Very well, lead on, my dear jailer. Together we shall ferret out justice from this tangle of tragedy!"

"Make way! Make way!" Bugbear snarled to the guards outside the jail as the tall woman escorted him onto the streets of Tiline. "Iawn Rhydd Cwestiwn here! Right of Free Question and all that rot! Official and perfectly legal! Now step aside! Step aside!"

"There's no sense in drawing undo attention," the tall woman said.

"And why not?" Bugbear said. "If I am to have special privileges, what is the harm in letting others know? Besides, I would be delighted if the true killer were to know of these developments. What is your name, by the by? I am called Bugbear, as I am certain you are well aware."

"Yes," the tall woman said with a sigh. "I am quite familiar with you, Lord High Advisor. My name is Zhora Ap Allherahiah."

"Ap Allherahiah?" Bugbear said, pausing in his steps and pulling away from Zhora. "That is the surname of the Dragon Brides! I shall not have one of your kind assisting me!"

"And what is it about 'my kind' that offends you so?"

"You are interfering, oppressive, and tyrannical!" Bugbear ranted. "You follow the dead dreams of a dead race - the dragons! And you foist these antiquated ideals upon the rest of the world whether welcome or not!"

"Are you quite finished?"

"Finished with you? Quite so!"

Bugbear turned about and commenced waddling away. However Zhora's stern, demanding hand quickly halted him and spun him about.

"Listen to me, little man," she hissed. "I was sent here by the Queen, who is a Dragon Bride herself. For some unfathomable reason, her husband the King thinks rather highly of you. She wanted me to insure that you did not cause any problems at the convention for his sake. And so that is what I shall do... and you shall cooperate. Is that understood?"

"You dare to order me about?" Bugbear said as he pulled away from the Dragon Bride. "Clearly as the King's Advisor, I outrank you! It is I who should be telling you what to do and how to do it!"

Zhora glared at Bugbear for several long, uncomfortable moments... her dark, piercing eyes never leaving his wide, saucer eyes... but her hand slowly moving under her cloak to the hilt of her broad sword.

"And that being the case," Bugbear said after loosening his red bow tie, "I demand that you assist me in my investigation!"

"As you wish, Lord High Advisor," Zhora said with a mocking bow and crooked smile.

Bugbear first targeted his fellow scholars for questioning. Most of them yet milled about the outdoor auditorium, swilling free tea and munching on truffles. But despite their accessibility the entire interviewing process proved to be quite an oratory ordeal.

"I was eating a truffle at the time!"

"I didn't see anything! And even if I did, I'd just as soon see you hang for the crime as anyone else!"

"...."

And that last comment was from a poor wretch who had taken a vow of silence, for so traumatized was he by Bugbear's tirade against De Sarno that he feared to ever speak again lest he make a grammatical error of his own.

"That was helpful!" Bugbear snorted as they wandered out of the auditorium. "The only thing we discovered is that they're out of truffles!"

"What about the coroner?"

"I don't imagine he has any truffles either."

"No!" Zhora said. "We could examine De Sarno's body ourselves."

"Ah! Excellent idea!" Bugbear exclaimed. "Come along then! Come along!"

Like a small, rotting toadstool, the coroner's office sprouted in the midst of the regal, high-spire churches, halls, and manors of downtown Tiline. The contrast was rather sickening... like seeing a baby rat squirming amongst newborn chicks. Bugbear dreaded knocking at the battered, wormwood door, fearing he might release some greater ugliness imprisoned inside that grotesque lump of a building. But knock he did, knowing that ugly or not, the truth was inside.

"Yes?" the coroner said, peeking through one of the worm-eaten holes. "What is it?"

"I wish to examine the corpse of Professor De Sarno," Bugbear replied.

"Impossible! He has already been cremated and his ashes scattered upon the back of a stray dog!"

"Why on earth would he want his ashes scattered on a dog?" Zhora said, her face contorted with disgust.

"He didn't," the coroner replied. "I tripped. Now if you'll excuse me, I have many important tasks to which to tend."

"May we at least see your report?" Bugbear asked, suppressing a bubbling impatience.

The coroner sighed. "Very well. You'll have to excuse the conditions," he said as he opened the door from the inside. "They don't allow much in the town budget for my office."

Bugbear and Zhora cautiously entered the ramshackle building. The walls were adorned with faded charts and diagrams portraying the anatomies of various races and animals. The furniture consisted of an examination table, several chairs, a desk, bookshelves, and strangely, a cot, indicating that the hovel was as much the coroner's home as it was his office. The only item of particular value in the decaying domicile was a finely woven, vibrant, rich, decorative rug... a recent addition as it carried no dirt, unlike the rest of the dust-drenched house.

"I recognize you!" Bugbear glowered. "You're the uncoordinated clod who ran into me at the marketplace this morning! The one who tangled me up in that very rug right there!"

"What of it?" the coroner said, straightening his stained and patched jacket, then taking a long swig from a whiskey bottle. "It's not like I poisoned someone with underdark root, now is it?"

Bugbear bitterly gritted his teeth and teetered back and forth, like a domino trying to decide if it should fall or stand.

"The report, if you please," Zhora said, placing a stabilizing hand on the goblin's shoulder.

The coroner smiled in a very false-faced way, taking a paper from the his desk and gingerly handing it to the Dragon

Bride. "Feel free to keep it. I have my own copy on file... as does the prosecutor."

"Excellent!" Bugbear piped. "The prosecution shall no doubt find it handy in prosecuting the true perpetrator of the crime!"

"Come along," Zhora said as she herded Bugbear out the door.

Out on the street Bugbear sputtered and fumed. "Where does a tattered, alcoholic ghoul like that find the nerve to address a goblin of my standing in such a manner?"

"Your public tantrums do nothing to help your case," Zhora said.

"True, true," Bugbear said, returning to a more congenial mood. "Now, let me see that report."

Bugbear looked through the paper letting out a series of *Aha's*, *Oh my's*, and *Well, well's*, followed by a long, drawn-out, *Hmmmmmmmmmm.*

"What does it say?" Zhora asked.

"That De Sarno is dead." Bugbear then shoveled the paper into his pocket.

"It doesn't look very good for your defense," Zhora sighed as they rested near the fountain in the town square.

"True," Bugbear said with finger poised thoughtfully at his chin. "But I can't help wondering... De Sarno must have made other enemies aside from me. That woman at the convention, the one who heckled him so, perhaps she is another suspect."

"Possibly," Zhora said with a nod. "Do you know who she is?"

"No," Bugbear answered. "But she used a particular term, 'nadredd.' I've heard it used before amongst certain sects of witches. I'd wager that we would find her at the local Witches' Lodge."

"An impressive piece of deduction," Zhora said.

"Your acknowledgment of my brilliance is duly noted," Bugbear said as he hopped off his perch on the fountain and tottered along the cobbled streets. "But don't let your blatant hero-worship interfere in your duties as my protector!"

"Oh, I think I can manage," Zhora said with thick layer of sarcasm as she followed the little man.

On the very end of Bob Bore Street in East Tiline stood the squat, thatch-roofed building known as the Witches' Lodge. It was a simple house, a mere two stories, with windows decorated in tasteful curtains and window boxes filled with vibrant, multi-colored flowers. The front door was made of solid oak with several ornate runes carved in intricate and complex patterns. And beside the door was a tall post with a rope attached to a bell.

"Now, let me handle this," Bugbear said. "Any interference from you would only contaminate my cautious and careful planning!"

Bugbear reached for the cord to ring the bell… but his lack of height made the task impossible. He looked to Zhora out of the corner of his eye, reaching up once again in an attempt to recover his dignity. But his stubby fingers fumbled just beneath the cord. Finally with a sigh he folded his arms. "Would you be so kind?"

"What?" Zhora said with a smirk. "And contaminate your cautious and careful planning?"

Bugbear's eyes narrowed with anger. "Very well," he hissed. With slow and determined movements he bent over and retrieved a small stone from the ground. Never taking his bitter gaze off Zhora, he flipped the stone towards the bell and produced a most satisfactory "clang!"

The heavy door creaked opened and a gray, wrinkled face peered out. "Faugh!" the old woman spat from her toothless mouth. "You should have been here two hours ago according to my tea leaves! But then again, it's so difficult to predict the comings and goings of goblins!"

Bugbear and Zhora stared at the old woman, eyes awash in curiosity and disbelief.

"The tea leaves said you'd stand around like idiots too," the old woman sighed. "Well, come in! Come in!"

Zhora and Bugbear cautiously entered the Witches' Lodge. Candles flickered in every direction, scattered throughout the room in apparent haphazard arrangement. Eerie shadows jumped upon the walls and ceiling. Yet strangely, there were no decorations, no symbols, no books... only the candles, three simple chairs, a table with a teapot and three cups, and a wood stove.

"Now, tell us what you know of De Sarno's murder," Bugbear said as he looked over the chair, which was quite large to one of his stunted height.

"De Sarno's fate is cloudy and uncertain to me," the old woman said, taking a seat and pouring a cup of tea.

"There's nothing cloudy about it," Bugbear said as he attempted to mount the overly large chair, trying to maintain his dignity while struggling and straining. "De Sarno is dead. And I have been implicated in his murder. And as I am innocent, that means someone else is guilty."

"And you suspect me?" the old woman cackled.

"I suspect everyone and everything," Bugbear said, his foot slipping off the support bar between the legs of the chair. He tumbled to the floor in a great hail of curses, thuds, and flailing limbs.

The woman's cackle rose through the lodge, louder and more mocking. "Perhaps the chair killed him?"

With a grumble and a stumble, Bugbear pulled himself to his feet, regained his composure, and glared at the old woman. "Laugh if you like…"

"Oh, I like! I like!"

"But I swear I shall find out who is to blame for De Sarno's death, and for framing me as the murderer!" Bugbear gripped his lapels in a gentlemanly manner and commenced a slow, pompous saunter about the table, his eyes never leaving the old woman. "You voiced your own distaste for De Sarno at the seminar, did you not?"

"Well, yes," the old woman said, her demeanor suddenly darkening.

"And why was that? What was it about De Sarno that enraged you so?"

"I wouldn't say enraged," the old woman replied. "Annoyed is a better word. And if you must know, it was his suspenders. Can't abide a man in suspenders."

"Suspenders, you say?" Bugbear said with upraised finger as he sauntered away from the table and towards the stove. "Are you certain that's it? Are you certain that perhaps it wasn't because De Sarno had discovered your taste for human flesh?"

"We witches have struggled for years to disprove such slanderous rumors!" the old woman protested. "We are not cannibals!"

"Is that so?" Bugbear said. The goblin paused for a few moments... letting a grin settle quite nicely into the creases of his face... his eyelids half-closing in a strange, surreal contentment. And then he opened the oven door with a dramatic flourish, displaying two young children sitting inside, faces covered in soot and bodies trembling. "Nothing says coven like someone in the oven."

"Those are neighborhood children the lodge has hired to clean the oven!" the old woman exclaimed with rolling eyes. "Ask their parents! They live right down the street!"

Bugbear looked to the children. They nodded in dumb agreement, seemingly more frightened by Bugbear's theatrics than anything else.

"Very well," Bugbear said with a crisp bow. "Everything seems to be in order here. Carry on! Carry on!" And with shameful head bowed, Bugbear quickly waddled out the door.

Zhora followed, giving the old woman an apologetic smile.

"That certainly turned out to be a red herring," Zhora said as she caught up to Bugbear out on the street.

"Indeed," Bugbear groaned. "And here I was hoping for a fish of an entirely different color after I'd heard those noises coming from the oven."

"Where to next?"

"I truly don't have a clue, my dear," Bugbear replied dejectedly as they wandered into the crowded marketplace. "We've tried everyone, everything, and every place."

"Except here," Zhora noted.

"The marketplace? Bah! Nothing here but rude venders and clumsy shoppers! Right over there is where the coroner and I...." Bugbear's words faded in his throat. The rug merchant. Something about him. Something strange. Strange about his hand. About the pinkie ring he wore.

Bugbear ran, his stubby legs moving in rapid, piston-like movements. "You there! Rug merchant! I say, where did you come upon that ring?"

The merchant looked to Bugbear as the goblin rushed up

to the booth. "Eh? You again? Well, if you must know, I took it as payment from that fella you got tangled up with this morning."

Zhora caught up to her charge. "If you run from me again like that, I'll have to kill you. Nothing personal."

Bugbear ignored the threat, concentrating instead on the series of sudden, brilliant inspirations that exploded in his brain. "With the rest of his home in such disrepair, why does the coroner have such a nice, and clearly expensive, rug? And isn't it rather suspicious that De Sarno was not only cremated, but that his ashes were 'accidentally' spilled on a stray dog? Now no one can examine the corpse or even the ashes. And the coroner's office was completely covered with dust. How is it that a coroner who has recently performed an autopsy has so much dust on his examination table and equipment? Our coroner friend is definitely hiding something! Therefore, there is only one thing to do!"

EPILOGUE 1

There was no warning. The door burst open, like all the winds of the North Sea had raged against it. De Sarno attempted to hide behind the crates in the basement, but it was too late... Bugbear and Zhora had already spotted him.

"In a basement, De Sarno?" Bugbear said, his tongue swimming in arrogance. "A fitting place for a worm like you!"

"How...?"

"You should be more cautious in your choice of bribe payments," Bugbear replied. "Your pinkie ring sticks out like a sore thumb. And you may consider improving the caliber of your underlings."

Zhora reached into the doorway and pulled a small, trembling, whiskey-soaked man into the room... the coroner.

De Sarno laughed. "Well, you've discovered my little ruse. But you must admit, I did prove my theories about the nature of perception and reality. Because of a simple slip of paper, everyone perceived that I was dead. And they perceived that you were the killer."

Bugbear joined in De Sarno's laughter. "Oh, yes! An excellent jest! And I must bow to your superior reasoning and scheming! If it weren't for the fact that you were ineligible, I'd nominate you for the Whittlegrip Fellowship!"

De Sarno's laughter bubbled and halted. "What do you mean, ineligible?"

"Well, the fellowship is only open to members of the Scholarly Council. And seeing as how you are deceased."

"But I'm not! I'm alive!"

Bugbear held aloft a pristine, white document. "I think not. According to this coroner's report, you are dead. You'll note this at the bottom here. It's the signature of the licensed coroner for this county. Makes the whole thing quite legal and binding. That's the funny thing about perception and reality, you see... both are dependent on paperwork!"

"I don't believe this," De Sarno screeched.

"And of course as you have no will and no living heirs, all of your lands, holdings, and valuables will be turned over to the King. And as I am the King's Advisor, I'm certain I can convince him that your estate would be best managed by myself. I would then perhaps be kind enough to let you live in the guest house... if you were to keep the shrubs trimmed. And I might even give you a generous allowance. Of course, the main house would be mine. I think I'll turn it into a gigantic rabbit hutch! Or perhaps a half-way house for runaway ogres!"

"Never!"

"Oh?" Bugbear said. "You don't like that idea, do you?" Bugbear removed another parchment along with a quill. "Then sign this and I'll destroy the death certificate."

De Sarno moved forward, his feet shuffling along the dirt floor in trepidation. He reached out for the paper. "What is it?"

"A contract. It states in no uncertain terms that you will surrender all scholarly and professorial duties and privileges until you successfully complete a course in remedial grammar at Willow Prairie University. Once you have completed the course, you shall be returned to your previous standing."

De Sarno looked at the contract with suspicious, roving eyes. Then he looked to Bugbear with equally suspicious, roving eyes. After a long moment of thought, his eyes softened. "Very well. I agree." De Sarno took up the quill and signed the document.

Bugbear received the paper and quill, quickly scrawling his

own signature, then looking at his prize with beaming pride. "Excellent! Excellent!" The goblin passed the paper back to Zhora. "Be so kind as to secure this, my dear. I shall entrust you to deliver it to the Royal Clerk in Willow Prairie." Bugbear then took up the death certificate. He held it before De Sarno, suspending the thin parchment betwixt the forefingers and thumbs of each hand. Then after several long, tense moments designed for racking nerves and making ulcers, Bugbear tore the certificate into quarters, handing them over to De Sarno.

De Sarno looked at the scraps of paper, the pale pall of desperation falling from his face, replaced by a smile of gratitude and relief. "Thank you! Thank you! I'll wire ahead to my manservant and make arrangements for enrollment immediately!"

"Yes, yes," Bugbear said with a scowl and dismissing wave of the hand. "Your toadying display grows tiresome almost before it begins. Away with you!"

De Sarno nodded with dumb agreement and hobbled out of the room.

"Well," Zhora said as she released the trembling coroner, who then scurried back up the stairs, "I must confess that I'm rather impressed. Not the most complex of mysteries, but still, you handled it rather masterfully."

"But of course," Bugbear said with a cocky, crooked smile. "And not only did I clear my name, but I eliminated a dangerous threat to the dignity and integrity of scholarship throughout the realm! For De Sarno shall never address another scholarly gathering as long as he lives!"

"What do you mean? If he enrolls in the grammar course..."

"He shall never enroll in the grammar course!" Bugbear erupted, an insane spark dancing along the corner of his eye. "For I am the chairman of the board of admissions for Willow Prairie University and I have full veto power! That fool may never learn to conjugate his verbs, but he shall learn to never again cross Bugbear!"

"Very strange," Zhora said, her eyes focused on the contract in a blatant attempt to avoid witnessing Bugbear's embarrassing tirade. "I was just glancing over your contract here and I've noticed something unusual."

"Don't tell me that twit De Sarno misspelled his own name!"

"No," Zhora said. "But do you see this line here where it says: 'And so the party of the first part and the party of the second part agree to put aside there differences."

Bugbear impatiently snatched the paper from Zhora's grasp, skimming down the page, his mumbling mouth following his dancing digit through the sea of words. "Yes, yes. I see it. What of it?"

Zhora took a deep breath and smiled the kind of smile folks reserve for those moments just before they lay a trump card, sink the final billiard ball, or serve a court summons. "You used the word 'there' spelled 'T-H-E-R-E', when I believe you meant to use the word 'their' which is spelled 'T-H-E-I-R'."

Bugbear blinked. And blinked again. He stared at the

impossible piece of paper... impossible because upon its smudged and crinkled surface his own words had turned against him.

"Bah!" Bugbear said, throwing the paper to the ground. "A minor error! I shall draw up a new contract and make De Sarno sign again! I'll tell him the old one was eaten by weevils!"

"I had something else in mind," Zhora said, a lazy finger thoughtfully stroking her chin.

EPILOGUE 2

"Mister Bugbear," Professor Hugo, instructor of the remedial grammar course, said in a sharp, condemning tone, "this is the second day of our course, and coincidentally enough, the second day you have been late!"

Bugbear winced. He took a moment to glare at his classmates, shaming their curious eyes back to their textbooks. Then with confident, determined steps he made his way from the doorway, past the small tables and chairs and awkward students, past the blackboard with its scrawled lessons, and finally to his own special chair and table near the front. "As was the case with yesterday," Bugbear said as he took his seat next to De Sarno and placed his satchel carefully atop the table, "I was detained by royal business. I assure you that my tardiness was unavoidable."

Professor Hugo nodded, his face sagging with sour agreement. "Well, I suppose I shall allow some leeway."

"Thank you," Bugbear sighed.

"Seeing as how there's extenuating circumstances."

"What?" Bugbear exploded, leaping to his feet and overturning his table, sending books, satchel, and papers flying.

The entire room went stone, dead silent... save for De Sarno who whispered quietly to himself: "Doesn't this nightmare ever end?"

The End

In Defense of Ogres

I ain't never seen a goblin afore that day. I'd heard some of the cowpokes talk about picking a few off out on the range, just for target practice. They always made it sound like they was killing prairie dogs or some such varmints. But this goblin looked all but human far as I was concerned. Sure he had pointy ears, a big pumpkin head, pug face, and skin like a worn leather saddlebag, but it was the proper way he carried hisself that made him seem more than just a varmint. In fact, he wore nicer clothes than me, all scaled down to fit his little three-feet tall self. Big red bow tie, nice neat green coat, yellow silk vest, clean pressed pants, and shiny buckled shoes. Lordy yes! I tells you that was one fancy dressed goblin! Course seeing how I was the town drunk, anyone this side of a pack mule would seems fancy dressed to me.

And the little cuss was sharp acting too! Like some kinda English royalty, full of fancy words and wild gestures. Watching him was like watching all of Shakespeare's plays at once!

"Step lively!" he barked to the stagehand as he waited for his luggage to be unloaded from the stagecoach. "I have important business here and I can't allow delay on account of sluggards like you!" A bold little pug! That stagehand was at least three times his size, but that goblin didn't pay no mind! He acted like he all but owned him!

Yes, sir, the day that goblin came to Chugwater was the day something special come into my life! Whether that special was specially fortunate or specially dangerous I still don't rightly know.

"You there!" the little feller said to me in his sharp, clear voice. "Where might I find the leader of this desolate, little town?"

I looked around, not quite sure if he was talking to me or some other folk. Being the town drunk, I wasn't used to being talked to... lessen it was wisecracks and insults. I propped myself up a bit higher, trying not to look like the type of folk what would be sitting on the ground as I was. "The hill," I said.

"And where might I find this hill'?" the goblin asked.

I looked around again, just to be sure he was still talking to me. "It's on the edge of town, 'bout three stumbles, five falls, and a long crawl."

The goblin laughed. Ain't never heard a sound like that afore. Kinda like a cat purring and a mule braying all together. And his mouth was all teeth. Big, flat, white teeth. I seen a picture in the paper once what looked like that laughing goblin. It was something called a car-toon.

"I can show you, if you want," I said.

"Yes, my dear fellow!" he said, trying to stop his laughing. "By all means, a delightful proposition!"

It took some doing. I'd been on quite a binge the night afore, so I was a bit shaky. But I led the little feller along at a good pace. I even took up his baggage for him. Awful heavy for such a little feller to be toting about.

Every bloodshot eye in the town turned as we walked down the boardwalk. They was used to me, sos I knowed they wasn't ogling me. They was looking... nope... they was glaring at the goblin.

You probably already know why folks was so down on goblins and other fey critters, but I'll give you the lowdown just in case you ain't as educated in such matters as I is.

I ain't exactly sure of the details, but there was a day back in 1899 when the world become a whole lot more bigger and a whole lot more complicated than all the teachers, preachers, and politicians could ever explain. They says all the critters from fairy tales, legends, and myths come spilling inta our world. Or that maybe we gone spilling inta theirs. Point is, suddenly us human folks was sharing our world with all these goblins, fairies, ogres, and so forth. You can imagine how wild things got. Never mind all the injuns, and blacks, and Irishmen. Suddenly the mean folks in the world had a whole new group to hate. Sad thing is, all the folks they used to hate, starting joining them in hating the new folks. So now we had all these wars going on. And governments all over the place started falling apart. Little kingdoms cropped up. Folks starting pulling in instead of spreading out. Lordy yes! It was a mess. Most folks starting calling the world "The Scatter Lands," just 'cause it seemed the best way to describe things.

Anyways, that was why all the folks started staring at the goblin. It was pure hate. Didn't faze the goblin though. He sauntered along like some little king parading down main street.

"My name is Bugbear, by the way," he piped to me. "By what name are you known."

"Call me Stubbins," I said, which only made sense as Stubbins was my name.

"Well, Mister Stubbins, I'll have need of an assistant while I'm here in Chugwater. I'm willing to pay quite handsomely. Twenty coppers a day, with a nice fat bonus when my business is completed. Are you agreeable?"

Twenty coppers could buy a lot of whiskey. "I'm agreeable... that is depending on what being an assistant is all about."

Bugbear chuckled. "I've been sent by King Martin the First of the United Realm of Willow Prairie. I'm here to retrieve Mister Tummer. I'll need someone to show me around town, run errands, and run interference."

"Lordy, Mister Bugbear!" I shouted without thinking. Then as I saw folks staring, I hushed it down a bit. "Ain't no way you're getting to Tummer, lessen you're part of the lynch mob. He's set for hanging sure as I'm set for drinking."

The goblin merely smiled. "I think I can put an end to both of those tragedies, my friend."

I was about to yelp more objections, but we'd found our way to the big house on the hill, where Boss Greetin lived. Boss Greetin ran Chugwater. Well, maybe ran ain't quite the word. Rode is more like it. And he rode her hard. He took everything he could from that town. His big mansion on the hill was proof to that. And it was him what started up the Dabbleworks, paying them dabblers to invent all sorts of weapons and such to make him powerful. No one could spit in that town without begging Boss Greetin first.

That's why Bugbear went to see him first. I begun to knock at the big double doors, but Bugbear pushed his way right on through, the doors opening before him like they was expecting him or some such thing. And how he got past all them guards without no one stopping him, I'll never know. It was like he'd put a spell on them. Next thing I knowed, we was sitting down in Greetin's study chatting away with him and Sheriff Werner like genteel high society folk.

"A trial?" Greetin laughed while he spewed big rings of smoke with his cigar. "Tummer is a killer. Worse, he's a child-killer. He doesn't deserve a trial. It's the gallows for him... as soon as my dabblers can build one strong enough to hold the ox."

Bugbear sat in a large, over-stuffed chair opposite Greetin. He seemed somehow uncomfortable there in all that luxury and splendor, like he'd rather be out-of-doors or in a regular home. But Greetin wasn't one to skimp on the good things in life. I could tell that as I sneaked some his brandy whilst he and Bugbear talked.

"This paper is an official writ from King Martin of the United Realm of Willow Prairie," Bugbear said, holding up a fancy looking piece of paper. "It authorizes me to act as Tummer's defense attorney."

The Sheriff was standing nearby, right at Greetin's right hand. After all, that's what peons was s'posed to do... stand by their bosses looking all surly and mean. I had me a particular dislike for that fat piece of trail flop. 'Cause he used to be my deputy when I was the Sheriff... until he spread lies about me and got me fired. You can imagine how I found my current career path not long after. Whiskey, wine, and other spirits is good for taking away every pain from bullet wounds to broken hearts and from toothaches to shattered dreams. Least that's what I thought at the time.

"You're crazy!" the Sheriff laughed. "First off, there ain't gonna be no trial! And second off, Chugwater ain't a part of your stupid 'United Realm of Willow Prairie'! Why would we care what your King Martin has to say, even if he is human?"

"Because," Bugbear said with real wide smirk, "the train route that brings the iron ore for Chugwater's Dabbleworks runs directly through the United Realm of Willow Prairie. That being the case, King Martin has every right to levy heavy tariffs on such transactions going across his borders. Or he might even halt such shipments altogether."

Lordy! Could that little cuss talk! Neither Werner nor me had a clue what he was talking about, even though we was both rightly impressed by the way he was saying it. The only one who seemed to understand was Greetin... and he didn't seem to care much for what he was hearing.

"Well, I suppose your King has every right indeed," Greetin said. "But why would he want to go and risk war over a piece of swamp rot like Tummer?"

"It's a matter of principle," Bugbear said.

Greetin closed his eyes and blew out a long stream of smoke. It was like he had them fancy words of Bugbear's inside his head and he was looking at them from all sorts of angles. Finally he chuckled. "I like your style, Mister Bugbear. I'll give you your trial. But on two conditions. I'm to be Prosecutor. And if I should win, you shall accept a permanent position in my administration. I'm sure I can beat what King Martin is paying you."

"An intriguing proposition," Bugbear said as he struggled from that big ol' chair. "I accept your conditions!"

Bugbear offered his hand to Greetin, and the thin scarecrow man stood and offered his, and then, of course, they shook hands, as was the custom.

"I'll arrange the trial for tomorrow," Greetin said.

"Excellent!" Bugbear piped. "Now, if you'll have your slovenly subordinate escort us to my client...."

Greetin snapped his fingers and Werner hopped to it... although he seemed none to happy about it.

I was in the midst of sampling some of Greetin's fine imported Scotch when Bugbear pulled me away. What poor timing. I could have gotten used to living like Greetin.

It was then that Werner first seemed to notice me. He gave a real wide grin as if to say: "Ain't I just better than you!" Well, I give him a look back what said: "You look at me like that again and you'll be picking your teeth off floor." His grin disappeared and he turned away from me, for Werner was a coward at heart, and was only able to face folks when their backs was turned.

All the posturing and poisoning concluded, we made our ways to the barn. The barn was a special place where the law kept the fey prisoners... ogres, dwarves, aes dana and what-not. They'd built it around two years ago after human folks in the area started having run-ins with such folks. It was all reinforced with concrete, surrounded by fences and barbwire, and guarded day and night by armed guards. Rumor has it they even had some of the inventors at the Dabbleworks whip up some special gadgets like electric fences and such.

Being the top law dog in the parts, Werner got us right through all the guards easy as easy could be. He led us through the halls, past the jail cells filled with goblin thieves, dwarven extortionists, aes dana con men, and redcap murderers. They even had scaled down cages for little pixie folk. But it was the big cages we was looking for. Only one of the big cages was currently occupied, and it was occupied by the most notorious criminal in the area... the ogre named Tummer.

He wasn't the vicious animal I expected. He sat all hunched over like a big hill of flesh and bone. Lordy yes! He was a big one! At least twelve feet tall and almost as wide! Big flat head, round black eyes, and big cauliflower ears. And he hummed some kinda song I ain't never heard afore. It was all soft and sweet and soothing. Reminded me of something a mother might hum to her baby.

"There he is," Werner said. "Just sits there humming. Can't even beat that damn hum outta him."

"For your information," Bugbear said, giving Werner a real cross look, "that is what ogres call 'The Great Song.' They believe that when God created the world, He used such a song. In that way, all things are connected through music." Bugbear moved up to the bars real slow-like. His big, saucer eyes went soft, like ice melting on a window pane. And then he started humming, just like Tummer. It was the most queer thing, hearing that big rumbling ogre voice and that little buzzing goblin voice all mixed together in the same, long, beautiful song.

"What the hell is he doing?" Werner asked.

"Harmonizing, you bonehead," I replied.

Suddenly Tummer stopped in his humming. He turned to look at Bugbear, a big old smile splitting his big, ugly face. "You hums good, little gobling," he said. "You comes for watchering them killering me?"

"No, Mister Tummer," Bugbear said. "I've come to get you out of here. But I'll need your help."

"Helpering you I will if'n it will be gettering me freed."

"Tell me what happened Tummer. Tell me about Cynthia."

It was as if Bugbear had just pulled a switch that shut off Tummer's brain. The big lug went all still and quiet, his face white and blank. He sat like that for a bit and then he trembled and sobbed.

"Take your time, Tummer," Bugbear said softly.

The ogre wiped away a couple of tears and started telling his story. "Cynthia was my friend, she was. Prettily little girls. Tiny and soft. She was teachings me all the things of words. Readings and writings and things of that sort. I'd carryings her on my shoulders through the swampses and we be laughering and playering all the day. Then one days I be comings into my home what was simply of mud and straw. And there I be seeing her, layings on the floor with bloods and spittles arounds her. I be thoughting she was comings to visit and sleeps while she waits for me. But no." He sobbed again. Lordy! It was like watching a volcano about to explode! So sad and pitiful. You'd never think the big monster was a child-killer for all the sorrow he showed. But then I never really believed all what they said about him anyhow.

See, Tummer was a local oddity. He lived in the swamps outside of Chugwater by hisself in a mud hut. Made his living catching catfish and selling them by the roadside. Passersbys was more likely to chuck rotten tomaters and more rotten insults at him than buy his fish. But, like a dumb dog what didn't know when it had been yelled at, he would just sit there with a big, dumb grin on his big, dumb face.

As far as I was concerned, Tummer was a harmless lug. He worked hard and made his own way, so that made him an all right feller in my book, even if he was as big as a boxcar. But when local children started turning up missing, Tummer become the first suspect. Werner and Boss Greetin was all hot to haul him in, but Judge Coyle wouldn't hear of it unless they brought back proper evidence. No sooner had the words left Coyle's mouth when Werner and his deputies found Tummer standing over little Cynthia's body. A tad too convenient, if'n you ask me. But no one asked me. Hell, once Tummer's gone, I'll be the bottom of the barrel in Chugwater society. Then maybe it will be me what's found standing over a dead body.

"Did you kill her, Tummer?" Bugbear asked. "We have to know. Even if it was an accident, you must tell us."

"No," Tummer said betwixt his sobs. "I loving Cynthia. She was me friend."

Bugbear turned to me and Werner. "He didn't do it."

Werner laughed. "That's the same line he's been giving us

from the get go! Obviously he's lying!"

"Ogres don't lie," Bugbear said. "They don't have the sophistication for such duplicities. They are simple and honest folk. And as for the other children, no one has found their bodies. So there is still some debate as to whether they are dead or simply missing. You have no case against Tummer."

I don't fully understand what Bugbear was saying, but by the time he was done saying it, he seemed a whole lot bigger and Werner seemed a whole lot smaller.

Bugbear turned away from the Sheriff and looked to Tummer. "Do not worry, Tummer. We shall get you a fair trial and I shall prove your innocence."

The ogre looked up from his sobbing, his little black eyes wet and glistening. "But will it be bringings back Cynthia?"

I thought I'd break down myself right there and then. So sad. No doubt in my mind, Tummer had been framed. And it didn't take no detective to know that Werner was involved.

"So what do we do next, boss?" I asked as we walked outta the barn and back towards the town proper.

"We sit back and see what kinds of doors we've opened," Bugbear said.

"What in tarnation is that s'posed to mean?" I said, all full of confusion and blustery, unsettled thoughts.

"You see, dear Stubbins," Bugbear started, "I have spent a good portion of my life studying the nature of things. In particular I have studied an ancient philosophy known as Non-Logical Thought. It is a philosophy devoted to working one's way around reality, warping the world to one's advantage, manipulating events in one's favor."

"And how in tarnation does one expect to do that?" I asked, dumb-founded as I was.

"It is really rather simple, my friend," Bugbear continued as we walked down the street past the gawkers, talkers, and balkers. "The world is full of locks. And each lock is opened by a different key. Werner is abusive yet insecure. And so I have unlocked him by treating him as an inferior. Greetin is greedy and ambitious. I have unlocked him by threatening his powerbase. Once you discover a person's combination, they are yours, dear Stubbins!"

I gave Bugbear a look what folks give when they feel they's being made a fool. "And what's my combination?"

He laughed. "No doubt you are tired of lugging my luggage about. And I imagine it has been some time since you've slept in a proper bed." He halted as if he was weighing his words. "Or since you've bathed in a proper bath."

I stopped and sniffed myself. For there wasn't nothing what got a man thinking about the way he smelt like when someone mentioned baths. And whew-eee! I was a horrible smell to behold! "I reckon you got that combination dead on."

And so we made way to the local tavern what also had rooms for rent. It was called "The Rusty Nail." A rowdy place, filled with rowdy folk doing rowdy things. There was some fuss from the barkeep about renting out rooms to a goblin and the town drunk, but when Bugbear pushed a hefty bag of gold across the counter to him, his tolerance improved a considerable bit.

Bugbear told me we was to freshen up, then meet down in the tavern. We'd eat and go over our plans for the trial. Beyond that, he didn't tell me nothing. And that was fine by me, as I had enough on my mind trying to remember how to shave.

I struggled something fierce with that tub! All them soaps and brushes and sponges and such! Didn't know what to do with which... but I muddled through. Clean is clean, after all, and when I dried off I was sure as clean as I'd been in a long time! Bugbear had even had some nice, new duds delivered to my room. By the time I was all done I looked like a proper gentleman with a fancy new jacket, snazzy new pants, jazzy new shoes, flashy new tie, and classy new look all-together!

After I got myself all gussied up, I hobbled downstairs, but Bugbear wasn't there yet. I took the opportunity to get me a drink... putting it on the goblin's tab, of course. Felt good to be sitting down at a table like regular folk, instead of dancing out on the floor hoping they'd toss a few pennies my way. Felt good to be clean too.

And the whiskey... that felt best of all. That warm tickle in my throat. That slow, spreading burn in my gut. That hallow, numbing buzz in my head. Lordy yes! It was a powerful good feeling, and I savored it most greedily.

Shortly Bugbear appeared. He didn't walk up or nothing. I just turned around and there he was... appeared! Like he done been there all along! Lordy yes! I'd have jumped out of my skin if I wasn't afraid of wasting a good bath!

"Terribly sorry," Bugbear said with a smile. "Didn't mean to startle you."

I was confused how he done such a thing. And thinking about it made me feel like someone was trying to clean out the inside of my skull with one of them scrub brushes. "Is this more of that Non-Logistical Thinking?"

"Non-Logical Thought," Bugbear chuckled. "Yes, it is. Perhaps after I've liberated Tummer I shall educate you further in this most illustrious science!"

We ate our suppers as Bugbear dictated. I had me a nice steak and potato, Bugbear a wedge of cheese and some strawberries. Best meal I'd had in quite some time. And I properly thanked Bugbear for such a treat. He was real gracious about it and said it was coming out of my pay. We both had quite a laugh over that... although I wasn't totally sure he was joking about it.

"Now then," Bugbear said, pulling a quill and paper from his vest, "let us commence our planning! First, what do we know?"

"Over twenty kids is missing. And one girl was found dead in Tummer's shack."

"What do we know about these children?" Bugbear asked.

"They was orphans," I replied. "Every last one of them. 'Cept Cynthia."

"Yes," Bugbear said, quickly scrawling something on his paper. "Orphans. And being orphans, they have no parents. And having no parents, they have no one to act on their behalf. So, my question to you is, who was it exactly who reported their disappearances in the first place?"

"Greetin. He started something he called a 'community adoption program.' He took all of these orphans in Chugwater and the surrounding towns and said he'd take care of them. I don't rightly know the specifics of where he kept 'em. All I know is that he said they suddenly showed up missing one day and then he started getting all hot to hang Tummer fer killing them."

"This is interesting," Bugbear said. "Very interesting. Greetin shall be one of our prime witnesses tomorrow, I assure you."

"You think he done it?"

"He is guilty of some crime, of that I'm certain. But I don't believe he is a child-killer. In fact, I don't believe the children are dead... yet. They have been kidnapped for a sinister purpose."

"What kind of purpose?" I asked.

Bugbear looked around like a dog looking around just afore it piddled on the good rug. He talked real soft to me. "My purpose for being here in Chugwater is two-fold, dear

Stubbins. I am to save Tummer. And I am to put a halt to the reawakening."

"Reawakening?"

Bugbear shushed me and looked around like he was gonna piddle again. "It is tradition in summoning rituals to spill innocent blood. When so many children suddenly went missing, King Martin and I immediately grew suspicious. It is our fear that someone is planning to reawaken something... evil"

I nodded like I understood. Even though I didn't. But I must have been as easy to read as a grade school primer, 'cause Bugbear started elaborating anyhow.

"We believe some evil force of unknown origin terrorized the world at the dawn of time, manipulating, murdering, and making a general nuisance of themselves. But the races united under the leadership of the Dragons and banished these creatures into the realm beyond the world. But it is entirely possible these evil beings made arrangements for their return. And there are certain disreputable types who would certainly welcome them!"

Again, I nodded like I understood. And again, I didn't.

Bugbear sighed, like a father what was trying to teach his blind son how to milk a cow. "Once there were some very, very bad people and they did very, very bad things until some very, very good people got rid of them."

"Oh!" This time I nodded and meant it.

"Now," Bugbear continued, "we have a list of what we know. What don't we know?"

"Where the children are and who took them."

"Exactly!" Bugbear started his jotting and scrawling again. "And what of Cynthia? How does she fit into this?"

"She was used to frame Tummer. Probably killed by Werner and planted in Tummer's shack under Greetin's orders."

"Excellent piece of deduction!" Bugbear said, raising his finger up and wagging it. "But entirely incorrect. You cannot let your personal distaste cloud your perceptions. Werner and Greetin lack the vision and intellect to mount such a scheme."

"Then that puts us right back where we begun!" I said with a frown.

"True," Bugbear said, rolling up his paper and shoving it in his pocket. "But unless you've begun, you'll never be done."

"That don't make no sense."

"But it's profound, so it doesn't need to make sense."

"My brain hurts."

Bugbear laughed. "Then it's time to retire for the evening. We have a big day tomorrow." Bugbear's eyes narrowed like the lids was the blinds on a shy man's windows. "And that day doesn't include drinking." He snatched up the bottle of whiskey I'd been drawing on and he handed it off to a waitress what was passing by.

I frowned. And I kept on frowning until Bugbear's own frown shamed me into looking away. "You're the boss."

Bugbear nodded. "The most intelligent observation you've made yet, Stubbins!"

Course he laughed again. Seemed like a pattern with him. But it wasn't like when other folks laughed at me. It was more like Bugbear laughed 'cause he wanted me to laugh with him.

I won't go into no detail on my sleep, 'cept to say that I had a nightmare about Tummer. He was clinging to a cliff edge and calling for me to haul him up. I tried. I tugged and pulled for all I was worth. But the big lug was too much for me. I watched and fretted as his fingers slipped from the edge, one by one. Then he fell. Seemed to be for miles. I turned about to get help, even as much as it was too late. But there stood little Cynthia, tears in her eyes... eyes that seemed to accuse me. Then I woke up. Couldn't get back to sleep again neither.

After I took me another bath (I could get used to such fine things), I met Bugbear outside the courthouse. He seemed pretty blasted calm for all the pressure what was on him. He may have thought Greetin didn't have much going in the scheming department, but as I was Sheriff under him once, I knowed the kinds of tricks he could pull. I was more than a little worried that weasel'd find some way to put Bugbear and me up on the gallows right aside Tummer!

We hurried ourselves inside and found our places at the

defense table. Soon Werner and his two deputies come tugging Tummer into the courthouse. There was a whole passle of folks swarming around them, jeering and hollering at Tummer. Tummer just shuffled on, his big shoulders round with sadness, his big arms and legs bound with logging chains, and his big, lumpy head bent down so it almost melted into his big, lumpy gut. They sat him down on the floor, for there wasn't no chairs big enough to hold all of hisself. Sitting there all hunched up like he was, he looked more like a child than a child-killer.

The jeering mob went on with a few more shouts and yips and yells, but soon they mostly shut themselves up as they took seats in the gallery.

Then in come Greetin. He was all dressed up in his fanciest duds… big bow tie, bright red vest, checkered jacket and pants, big top hat, and silver handled cane. He was a sight. Best-dressed scarecrow I ever seen! He took hisself to the prosecutor's table, giving Bugbear a sly wink afore he sat down.

One of the deputies took his place by the judge's bench and cleared his throat. "All stand for the honorable Judge Coyle."

And so we all stood, although Bugbear could hardly see over the table as short as he was, and Tummer made a horrible racket with his chains.

Judge Coyle come into the room like some actor taking the stage. He twirled his black robe and smiled wide as could be.

Most folks liked Judge Coyle. He wasn't no real judge. No proper schooling for the job or nothing of the like. But he was a nice feller and a fair man, so folks kept electing him. And he sure did like to clown around and carry on with flowery words and phrases. I think he was from England or one of them other exotic countries where it was normal to act so strange.

"Well, well, well!" he said as he sat at the bench and moved his hands to let folks know they could sit too. "What a surprise this is! The way everyone was carrying on I thought we would have the execution before the trial!"

Boss Greetin stood with a fake, salesman's smile plastered on his ugly pug mug. "Why, your Honor, certainly you realize that the people firmly support justice, no matter how unnecessary it might be."

"Yes," Coyle said. "It's quite touching, the way you and your cronies have leapt into the arena of public service. Rather like foxes leaping into the arena of rabbit preservation."

A few people chuckled, but most seemed a bit put-off. Bugbear himself seemed too wrapped up in his notes and scribbles to pay much mind to anything else.

"Let's get on with this," Coyle sighed. "Opening arguments. We'll start with the great humanitarian, Mister Greetin."

Greetin stood up and you could tell by the way he puffed out his chest he was offended by Coyle. But he didn't say nothing about it, for Coyle was so popular, and a popular person could be as scary to a tyrant as a gun to the head. "Your

Honor and distinguished guests, the people intend to prove beyond a shadow of a doubt that the defendant, Tummer the ogre, is guilty of kidnapping and murder. To prove this we shall present overwhelming evidence of the defendant's guilt. We shall present the expert eyewitness testimonies of law enforcement officials and community leaders. We shall remind the court of the innocence and purity of the victims of this crime. And we shall remind the court that the town has already gone to a considerable expense to build a special gallows. Thank you." Greetin bowed and sat down.

Coyle nodded to me and Bugbear. "The defense may present its opening arguments."

Bugbear stood and walked around afront of the table. He cleared his throat as if making room for profound things. Then he spake: "Tummer is innocent." Then he move back to his seat and sat down.

Course, everyone seemed a bit alarmed and disappointed that that was all Bugbear had to say. But the little cuss sure seemed confident that he'd done said something important.

"Ain't you gonna say no more?" I asked.

Bugbear shook his head. "Talking gets in the way of listening," he whispered.

"I don't understand."

"Then start listening."

Coyle pounded his gavel to keep the folks in the gallery

from mumbling so. Then he pointed to Greetin and sighed. "Call your first witness."

"I call Sheriff Werner," Greetin said.

The bloated sack of sorghum waddled up to the stand. His deputy held up a Bible for him to swear on. Almost seemed a sin in itself to have a devil like Werner swearing his oath on the Good Book. But he did and sat his big double-wide rear in the chair.

"Sheriff Werner," Greetin begun, "would you please describe the events of August third."

"Uh, all of them?" Werner asked.

Greetin rolled his eyes, and you could tell he wished he'd made a better choice in lap dogs. "No. Tell the court about what you found at Tummer's shack that day."

"Oh. Well, me and my deputies found little Cynthia Drake dead on the floor."

"In your expert opinion, what killed her?"

"Tummer."

"Thank you, Sheriff. No further questions." And Greetin sat down with a really cocky smile on his face.

Coyle looked to Bugbear. "Your witness."

Bugbear stood and walked around to Werner, his hands on his lapels in a very official looking pose. "Tell me, Sheriff," he said, throwing in one of them long dramatic types of pauses lawyers is so fond of, "what was Tummer's demeanor when you found him?"

Werner waddled in his seat a bit like he'd done messed in his drawers. He looked up to the Judge. "Uhm, what's demeanor?"

"His mood," Bugbear jumped in. "His attitude. How did he act when you found him and told him about Cynthia's death."

"Well, he seemed mighty upset. He started bawling and all."

"He cried? Like he was suffering a loss?"

"Objection!" Greetin said. "Council is leading the witness."

"Well someone needs to lead the twit!" Bugbear said. "Otherwise we'll never get anywhere with him!"

The gallery laughed a bit at this, although some seemed a bit afraid of offending Werner.

Coyle chuckled a bit too. But he soon pounded that gavel of his again. "Objection sustained."

Bugbear bobbed from side to side. He looked like some kind of little teapot what was boiling over. Then he bottled up all that steam and turned back to the table. "No further questions."

The crowd mumbled some more as Werner waddled hisself off the stand.

"The prosecution may call its next witness," Coyle said.

And so Greetin called his next bootlicker, and another. And each one couldn't answer most of Bugbear's questions on account of Greetin's objections and Coyle's sustainings. I was beginning to think that Coyle wasn't such a nice feller after all. Maybe he was in Greetin's pocket just like everyone else, and me and Bugbear was the only honest folk in the whole blamed town.

Finally it come to Bugbear's turn to call witnesses.

"The defense has only one witness, your honor." Bugbear pulled out another one of them dramatic pauses. Everyone was as on edge as cats in a kennel. "We call Boss Greetin to the stand."

Of course there was a gasp. Couldn't call the man what owned to town without everyone gasping. Would have been rude to do otherwise.

"Objection, your Honor!" Greetin yelled.

"Overruled!" Bugbear yelled in reply.

Coyle shook his head and sighed. "Council, it is highly irregular to call the prosecutor to the stand. Would you care to explain yourself?"

"Certainly!" Bugbear piped. "As Mister Greetin is the legal guardian of the missing children, he is as much a suspect as the defendant."

"Preposterous!" Greetin shouted.

Coyle pounded that gavel of his again. "I'll decide what and who is preposterous in this courtroom, Mister Greetin! Mister Bugbear makes a valid point. I shall allow his request."

Greetin was powerful mad about the whole thing, but he complied. I could hear him whisper to Bugbear as he walked up to the stand. "I thought you was smart, little man. But you're throwing your life away."

"No," Bugbear said. "I'm throwing this trial right back in your face."

Greetin sat down in the chair real hard, like a kid what was pouting 'cause his mama wouldn't give him his chocolate pudding. He went through all the oath-taking and so forth, and then the questions commenced.

"Mister Greetin," Bugbear started, "where are you keeping the children?"

"Objection!" Greetin shouted.

"Overruled!" Bugbear shouted.

"Council," Coyle sighed, "will you kindly allow me to do the overruling?"

"Of course," Bugbear said. "Profuse apologies, your Honor."

Greetin smiled like a cat with a mouthful of mouses.

"Objection overruled."

Them mouses must have turned real sour all the sudden, 'cause so did Greetin's expression.

"Answer the question, Mister Greetin!" Bugbear demanded.

"I'm not keeping the children!" Greetin screamed. "I don't know where they are!"

"Where did you last see them?"

Greetin paused. "I don't want to answer that."

Tummer started humming. Slow and low at first. Only me and a few other folks could hear.

"Please, Mister Greetin," Coyle said. "It's a fair and relevant question. Answer it."

Tummer hummed louder. More folks started hearing it and they started staring at him.

"They were in their room," Greetin said.

"Their room?" Bugbear said. "And where was their room?"

The humming was powerful loud now. Everyone turned to look at the big ogre. He just kept humming like that was all there was to life. Then he stood up. The deputies went for their guns as the crowd commenced to gasp and scream. But Tummer swatted them aside afore they had a chance to do anything to stop him. He broke them chains like they was made of paper. Then he started shambling out the door, paying not a mind to no one as he hummed his song.

Werner started waddling after the ogre, yelling and hollering to his deputies. But Bugbear was faster. He bolted after Tummer, and he shouted out to me as he passed by. "Stubbins! Come along! Things have finally gotten interesting!"

I'd thought things was interesting enough afore, but I followed Bugbear anyhow. Soon after the entire courthouse emptied out, running after Tummer as he lumbered down the street. Lordy! He had a stride, he did! Like one of them big old gee-raffs from Africa. He out-paced the whole lot of us. But we could all keep him in sight. And the whole time he was humming.

The chase ended at the Dabbleworks. We found Tummer, sitting there outside, humming as he had been, but not moving at all. Werner and his men leveled their ogre rifles (what was really buffalo rifles with a bit of extra kick dabbled into them.) The crowd cowered away as they knew what was coming next. Bugbear moved to stop them from doing the poor slob in.

But then the most amazing thing happened. The kids come out of the Dabbleworks, just as spry and alive as could be. Smiling. Laughing. Carrying on like little kids was supposed to.

All the folks gathered around, Greetin, Werner, and Coyle included.

"The Great Song!" Bugbear gasped. "It worked! Tummer found them through the song!"

"I don't understand," Greetin gasped. "They were missing. We searched all over the complex for them."

Bugbear shot Greetin a glare what said every mean word in

the world all at once. "So! You were keeping the children here as cheap labor for your Dabbleworks!"

Greetin hung his head like a whipped dog. "Yes. But they were missing. Gone. Vanished. Where did they come from?"

"From the truth," a boy said, stepping away from the other kids. "You worked us like animals, Boss. Till one day when we found a hunk of ore with all sorts of writing on it, a remnant of something old and powerful! And then we started hearing voices. The voices told us what to do. Told us to hide in the deepest parts of the Dabbleworks. Told us how to make ourselves invisible. Told us to murder Cynthia Drake and frame Tummer."

"Tummer!" Bugbear shouted. "Tummer was the innocent sacrifice!"

"Very good!" the boy said. "And I imagine he would have been dead by now and our new guardians would be running things if it wasn't for your interference."

Lordy! That kid was talking almost as fancy as Bugbear! Whatever them voices had been telling him, they must've been feeding him with all sorts of big words too! The rest of them kids started gathering around Tummer. They had knives! Hellfire! I think they was going to kill him! And no one was going to lift a finger to help that big, dumb ogre. We all just stood their staring, watching them little children stalking like regular full-growed thugs.

"Since it seems you can never count on grown-ups to do

anything for you," the boy said, "we'll sacrifice Tummer ourselves."

Bugbear run forward, yelling and hollering as he stepped afore Tummer to protect him from the kids. I didn't have nothing better to do, so I done the same, holding Bugbear by the shoulders to keep him from doing nothing what would get hisself killed any faster. And the whole time Tummer was humming. Not doing a blamed other thing but humming.

"You found that Cynthia wasn't enough!" Bugbear said. "A little girl only had enough innocence to allow your evil benefactors to possess you. But Tummer... Tummer will give them the power they need to fully manifest!"

"Yes, yes, yes," the boy said, acting all of the little growed-up jackass. "We all know how clever you are, goblin. Now, step aside and let destiny unfold!"

Just as them dagger blades was just inches from us, them children stopped. Tummer's humming was even louder, and them little kids started shaking and trembling along with his song.

"What in tarnation?" I shouted.

"The Great Song!" Bugbear said. "Tummer is using it to draw the evil influence into himself!"

And sure enough, all twenty of them ragamuffins fell to the ground, these big, red clouds coming out of them and streaking towards Tummer. They shot right into Tummer like bullets into dead meat. Then he doubled up like he had hisself a powerful gut ache. But he still kept on humming while he rolled in the dirt.

Bugbear moved back and urged me to follow. We gathered about the rest of the townsfolk, while some of the women and the town doctor tended to the fallen children. We all stood and looked at each other. Bugbear, Coyle, Greetin, Werner, and myself. Finally Bugbear started humming along with Tummer. Lordy! I'll be buttered and fried if that big ol' ogre didn't start a glowing! Bugbear hummed louder. I didn't know what else to do, so I joined in. Then Coyle, he started humming too. Then the barkeep. The undertaker. The ranchers. The widows and widow-makers. Even Greetin and Werner joined in after a bit of nervous twitching and wondering.

And Tummer kept on squirming and flailing in the dirt, and all the while his big, throaty voice kept on humming. That big red glow got bigger and redder. And all of us hummed louder and louder. I couldn't hear it too well, as my own humming filled most of my head, but I could imagine it would have been quite a sound, all of them people humming the same beautiful song. It must have done some good too, 'cause that red glow started pulling away from Tummer like an ugly butterfly pulling away from its cocoon. Bugbear danced around in front of everyone, urging us to hum louder, raising his arms and flailing them around like mad. And we done hummed our hearts out. And the red glow done shot up into the sky, voices screaming from it as if there was people inside being ripped into pieces. It shimmered afore us a bit longer, and then it faded away like smoke in the wind.

Most everyone was dumb-founded by what they'd just seen. But Bugbear walked up to Tummer's still body. I followed, a bit more skittish-like than my boss. The goblin bent down and listened at the ogre's chest. He pulled away, looking all serious to the crowd. And he shook his head. We all knew what it meant. We all knew that the strain had been too much for him. He was dead.

Bugbear turned back to Tummer and picked up a book what was clutched in the ogre's hand. I couldn't read it myself, but it looked to be a grade school primer. Bugbear opened it to the first page where there was something scrawled there like it was done by a two-year-old.

"Tummer and Cynthia is friends," Bugbear read aloud.

I swear, every person there started to bawl when they heard that. Whether it was guilt for what they done to Tummer, or sadness over what happened to Cynthia, or whatever... they was crying like newborns. Even Werner got misty over the whole thing. For all the good our tears done poor Tummer now.

Chugwater was a changed town after Tummer died. Greetin was chased out of town all together. The big house was put to good use though, as a new orphanage and reform school for the kids. And we brought in real workers to take over their jobs in the Dabbleworks. We elected Coyle as Mayor. Werner lost the Sheriff election to yours truly, after I kicked my drinking habit, that is. And I got me some honest deputies in there to help me sort through the barn on who belonged there and who was innocent.

But the nicest things we done was built a statue of Tummer and Cynthia. It was every bit as big as the ogre hisself, with Cynthia sitting all pretty and happy on his lap, reading to him. It was made of the best bronze the Dabbleworks could turn out. And at the bottom of the statue was the words: "Tummer - Friend of Children."

I never saw Bugbear again. But we sure did see lots more other goblins, and ogres, and dwarves, and such, as Chugwater became a part of the United Realm of Willow Prairie, and a proper integrated society.

Yep. I knowed that goblin was going to stir things up when he come to town. I just never realized till now how much stirring we really needed.

The End

Bugbear's Journal

Day of the Bitter Donkey, Year of the Endless Question,
Age of the Forgotten Hive
September 25, 1900 - by human reckoning

After spending considerable time searching for answers among human settlements, I have decided to pursue the more risky strategy of venturing into Áes dána territory. This is particularly dangerous as I am entering King Brenen's lands. Unlike his more practical and even-tempered cousins, Brenen refused to sign the non-aggression treaties with King Martin. If I am caught, I shall have no defense, diplomatic or martial.

I am particularly fearful of being laid low by an Áes dána arrow.

History tells us that even as the Nagonene archers were feared for their stealth and speed in battle, the regal Áes dána bowmen were renowned for their accuracy and efficiency. It was said a Nagonene could kill a man at 200 yards, while an Áes dána could split the Nagonene's arrow before the body hit the ground. Indeed, there was something of a rivalry between the Migatwik and the Bogha Laoch' during the first war against the Shadow Smith.

The results of this competition vary, but it is generally considered that while the Migatwik had the higher kill rate, the Bogha Laoch tended to make more difficult shots at greater distances.

Unlike the Migatwik, the Bogha Laoch are still with us, although over the years their ranks have become more devoted to tournaments and pageantry than combat. Still, I fear the sting of their arrows more than that of a human rifle or pistol, for modern human weapons can never match the brutal elegance of a well-shot arrow.

[1] An elite regiment of Áes dána archers.

If you've enjoyed this book, be sure to stop by www.nogglestones.com for more information about *Noggle Stones*. We'll have lots of updates about the books, as well as archery line, card game, role-playing game, audio drama, and more!

NOGGLE STONES™
YOUTH ARCHERY GEAR

PREMIUM WOOD ARROWS

Designed after the arrows used by the Nagonene warriors and the Dragon Brides from the pages of Noggle Stones™. These wood arrows are made with premium wood shafting and 3-fletched with a unique, fantasy style cut real turkey feather.

Riley Ratcatcher

Maga Ap Allherahiah

BOW OF THE NAGONENE

An officially licensed Noggle Stones™ Youth Archery product, this bow is all Hickory, hand-crafted, and very affordable. A perfect bow to get your young archer involved in the sport.

www.ingramcontent.com/pod-product-compliance
Lightning Source LLC
Chambersburg PA
CBHW071338130626
46556CB00004B/1936